·LIONEL·
IN THE FALL

·LIONEL·
IN THE FALL

by Stephen Krensky
pictures by Susanna Natti

PUFFIN BOOKS

For Andrew
S. K.

To Max and Bea
S. N.

PUFFIN BOOKS
Published by the Penguin Group
Penguin Books USA Inc., 375 Hudson Street, New York, New York 10014, U.S.A.
Penguin Books Ltd, 27 Wrights Lane, London W8 5TZ, England
Penguin Books Australia Ltd, Ringwood, Victoria, Australia
Penguin Books Canada Ltd, 10 Alcorn Avenue, Toronto, Ontario, Canada M4V 3B2
Penguin Books (N.Z.) Ltd, 182–190 Wairau Road, Auckland 10, New Zealand

Penguin Books Ltd, Registered Offices: Harmondsworth, Middlesex, England

First published in the United States of America by Dial Books for Young Readers, 1987
First paperback edition published by Dial Books for Young Readers, 1989
Published in a Puffin Easy-to-Read edition, 1993

7 9 10 8

Text copyright © Stephen Krensky, 1987
Illustrations copyright © Susanna Natti, 1987
All rights reserved

LIBRARY OF CONGRESS CATALOGING-IN-PUBLICATION DATA
Krensky, Stephen.
Lionel in the fall / by Stephen Krensky;
pictures by Susanna Natti.   p.   cm. — (Puffin easy-to-read)
"Reading level 2.0"—T.p. verso.
"First published in the United States of America by Dial Books
for Young Readers, 1987"—T.p. verso.
Summary: For Lionel, fall means starting a new school year,
raking leaves, and getting to dress up as a knight and
chase a dragon from house to house on Halloween.
ISBN 0-14-036545-1
[1. Autumn—Fiction. 2. Halloween—Fiction.]
I. Natti, Susanna, ill. II. Title. III. Series.
[PZ7.K883Lk 1993]
[E]—dc20   93-6554   CIP   AC

Reading Level 2.0

CONTENTS

BACK TO SCHOOL

Lionel was getting dressed
for the first day of school.
He put on his new shirt
with the stiff buttons.
He pulled on his new pants.
He tied his new shoes tight.
Then he went downstairs.

Everyone else was in the kitchen.

Father was making eggs.

Mother was drinking coffee.

His big sister Louise

was eating cereal.

"Have some breakfast," said Father.

Lionel didn't want anything.

He just pushed his egg around.

"What's the matter?"

asked Mother.

"I have a new shirt, new pants,
and new shoes," said Lionel.

"But I am just the same old me.
I don't match my new things."

"That's dumb, Lionel," said Louise.
"Even for you."

Lionel ignored her.

"Everything looks like it matches,"
said Father.

"Well, maybe we should check,"
said Mother.

She opened her purse.

"What are you doing?" asked Lionel.

"You'll see," said Mother.

She took out a picture

and a small mirror.

She gave the picture to Lionel.

"Who's that?" asked Mother.

"It's me," said Lionel.

"You took it last year

on the first day of school."

"That was the old you," said Mother.

She held out the mirror.

"This is the new you," she said.

Lionel looked in the mirror.

Then he looked down

at his arms and legs.

"Everything is longer," he said.

"And my face is not so round."

"You're bigger and stronger now,"

said Mother.

"You match your new things perfectly."

Lionel gobbled up his egg.

"Why are you eating so fast?"

asked Father.

"I have to get to school,"

said Lionel.

"The new me doesn't want

to be late."

THE NEW TEACHER

Lionel knew everyone in his class.

And everyone knew him.

But nobody knew the new teacher.

"Good morning," she said.

"I am Mrs. Banks."

"Good morning, Mrs. Banks,"

said the class.

Mrs. Banks nodded. "It's nice
to meet you all," she said.
"I'd like to know you better.
Please stand up and tell me
a little bit about yourselves."

Jason was first.

He talked about his pet turtle.

His words came out so fast
they all ran together.

Emily was next.

She talked about her last baseball game.

Her voice sounded higher than usual.

"What about you?" said Mrs. Banks.

She was pointing at Lionel.

Lionel scraped his chair back

as he stood up.

"I'm Lionel," he whispered.

His face turned pink.

"Speak up," said Mrs. Banks.

The pink darkened to red.

"I'm Lionel," he whispered again.

Mrs. Banks shook her head.

"You must speak louder," she said.

"We all want to hear you."

Lionel was now red enough to explode.

"I'M LIONEL!" he shouted.

"AND I HATE STANDING UP HERE

TALKING IN FRONT OF EVERYONE!"

Lionel sat down. He bit his lip.

The class was completely still.

Everyone wondered what
the new teacher would do.
Sarah thought Mrs. Banks would
yell back at Lionel.
Jeffrey thought she would
send Lionel to the principal.

But Mrs. Banks didn't yell.

And she didn't send Lionel anywhere.

She only smiled.

"When I was your age, Lionel,"

Mrs. Banks said,

"I hated to stand up and talk too.

I had forgotten that.

Thank you for reminding me."

She passed out paper to the class.
"All of you can write me
about yourselves instead."
Lionel took out his pencil
and began writing.
He had a lot to say.

RAKING LEAVES

Lionel was raking leaves

in his backyard.

The leaves were red

and yellow and brown.

The ground was covered with them.

Lionel raked and raked and raked.

His arms got sore.

His legs got tired.

Louise came outside wearing a dress.

She was going to a birthday party.

"Keep up the good work, Lionel,"

she said. "Maybe you'll be done

by Thanksgiving."

She kicked up some leaves and left.

Jeffrey passed her on the driveway.

"Hi, Lionel," he said.

Lionel was glad to see him.

Jeffrey was tall.

He was strong.

Jeffrey could be a big help.

"Nice day," said Lionel.

Jeffrey looked at the yard.

"Too bad you have so much to do,"
he said.

"It's worth it," said Lionel.

"I'm building the biggest pile
of leaves in the world."

Jeffrey laughed.

"Really," said Lionel.

"It will be this big," he said.

He opened his arms wide.

"And it will be fun

to jump in when I'm done."

Jeffrey nodded. "Can I jump too?"

"If you want," said Lionel.

"Of course, I have to finish

raking first."

Jeffrey looked around.

"There are a lot of leaves here,"

he said.

"How long will it take you?"

"A long time," said Lionel.

"Maybe weeks."

Jeffrey smiled.

"I don't believe you," he said.

Lionel started raking again.

"Well, it will take a while," he said.

"And I'm working as hard as I can."

Jeffrey wrinkled his nose.

"You would get done faster

if I helped," he said.

"That's true," said Lionel.

"Maybe even today," said Jeffrey.

"Maybe," said Lionel.

"Do you have another rake?"

"In the garage," said Lionel.

Lionel and Jeffrey worked hard
for a long time.

By late afternoon all the leaves
were in one huge pile.

Lionel and Jeffrey jumped in it
lots of times before dark.

TRICK OR TREAT

It was Halloween night.

Lionel was going out as

a knight in shining armor.

His father was going out as his horse.

Lionel had made the armor with

cardboard and foil.

His horse was covered with

a sheet and a paper bag.

Lionel and his horse

went out into the night.

It was very dark.

The moon was very bright.

Monsters and clowns were running
through the neighborhood.
Lionel was not afraid.
He had his armor and his trusty horse
to protect him.

At the first house

a man opened the door.

"Trick or treat," said Lionel.

"I am here to fight the dragon."

The man gave Lionel a candy bar.

"A dragon was here a minute ago,"

he said. "Maybe you can catch it."

Lionel hadn't expected this.

Who could this dragon be?

Jeffrey? Sarah? Benjamin?

His horse didn't know.

"But maybe you can find this dragon,"

he said.

Lionel ran across the street.

A woman opened the door.

"Trick or treat," said Lionel.

"I am here to fight the dragon."

The woman gave him a candy bar.

"You just missed it," she said.

"Try next door."

Lionel and his horse

went from house to house.

They passed witches and ghosts

and clowns and robots,

but no dragons.

Lionel looked for dragon prints

in the grass.

He didn't find any.

Once Lionel thought he heard

the dragon growling in the distance.

His horse had heard something too.

"Where are you, dragon?"

shouted Lionel.

The dragon didn't answer.

Lionel finally gave up

and took his horse home.

The dragon was waiting for them
in the living room.
It had large green scales
and wings like a giant bat.
"Grrrrrr," roared the dragon.
"Uh-oh," said his horse.
"I think we found it."

But Lionel knew that roar.

"You!" said Lionel.

"You were the dragon, Louise."

Louise took off her dragon's head.

"Yes," she said.

"And you couldn't catch me all night."

Lionel dropped his bag of candy.

"Well, I'll catch you now,"

he said.

And he chased her all

over the house.